Memories
of the
MANGER

This book is for

_____

Memories
of the
MANGER

Written by Michelle Medlock Adams

Illustrated by Doris Ettlinger

ideals children's books.
Nashville, Tennessee

ISBN 0-8249-5476-9

Published by Ideals Children's Books
An imprint of Ideals Publications
A division of Guideposts
535 Metroplex Drive, Suite 250
Nashville, Tennessee 37211
www.idealsbooks.com

Color separations by Precision Color Graphics, Franklin, Wisconsin

Printed and bound in Italy by LEGO

ALSO BY MICHELLE MEDLOCK ADAMS
Conversations on the Ark
The Sparrow's Easter Song
My Funny Valentine
Little Colt's Palm Sunday

10 9 8 7 6 5 4 3 2

Designed by Eve DeGrie

To Susie McGregor—Thanks for being such
a wonderful friend and sister in Christ.
Love ya! —Michelle "Missers" Medlock Adams

To the children of St. Peter's, Washington, New Jersey
—Doris Ettlinger

Library of Congress Cataloging-in-Publication Data

Adams, Michelle Medlock.
  Memories of the manger / written by Michelle Medlock Adams ;
illustrated by Doris Ettlinger.
     p. cm.
  ISBN 0-8249-5476-9 (alk. paper)
  1. Jesus Christ—Nativity—Juvenile fiction. I. Ettlinger, Doris. II. Title.
  PZ8.3.A215Me 2005

                          2005003115

And she brought forth her firstborn son,
and wrapped him in swaddling clothes,
and laid him in a manger; because there was
no room for them in the inn. —Luke 2:7

The donkey called from down below,
"We're ready, Mrs. Dove!
Please tell your story once again,
The one about God's love."

The old dove stretched her wings out wide
And cooed a gentle coo.
"I'll be right down," the dove called out,
And all at once she flew.

She landed on the donkey's back
And then hopped to the ground.
The animals all moved in close.
Nobody made a sound.

The colt, the lamb, the kid, the chick,
The mouse and donkey too—
They all had heard the tale before,
But each time it seemed new.

"It happened here, right in this barn,"
The old dove softly said.
"The Son of God was born right here,
Upon this small straw bed.

"This nice young couple came to town,"
The dove said with a grin.
"But Bethlehem was all filled up—
No rooms in any inn!

"The woman wanted to relax.
The time was drawing near.
She really needed to give birth.
That's why they came in here.

"She was so young, so beautiful,
And Mary was her name.
Somehow I knew when she gave birth,
I'd never be the same.

"And then it happened, just like that.
I heard the baby's cries.
She pulled her baby close to her
And looked into his eyes.

"She said, 'Jesus will be your name,
Just like the angel said.'
And then she smiled and praised our God,
And kissed the baby's head."

"What did he look like?" asked the colt.
"Was he real big and strong?
And why'd he cry? Was he OK?
Or was there something wrong?"

"No, he was perfect," said the dove.
"At birth, all babies cry.
When you were born you neighed and neighed.
I'm really not sure why.

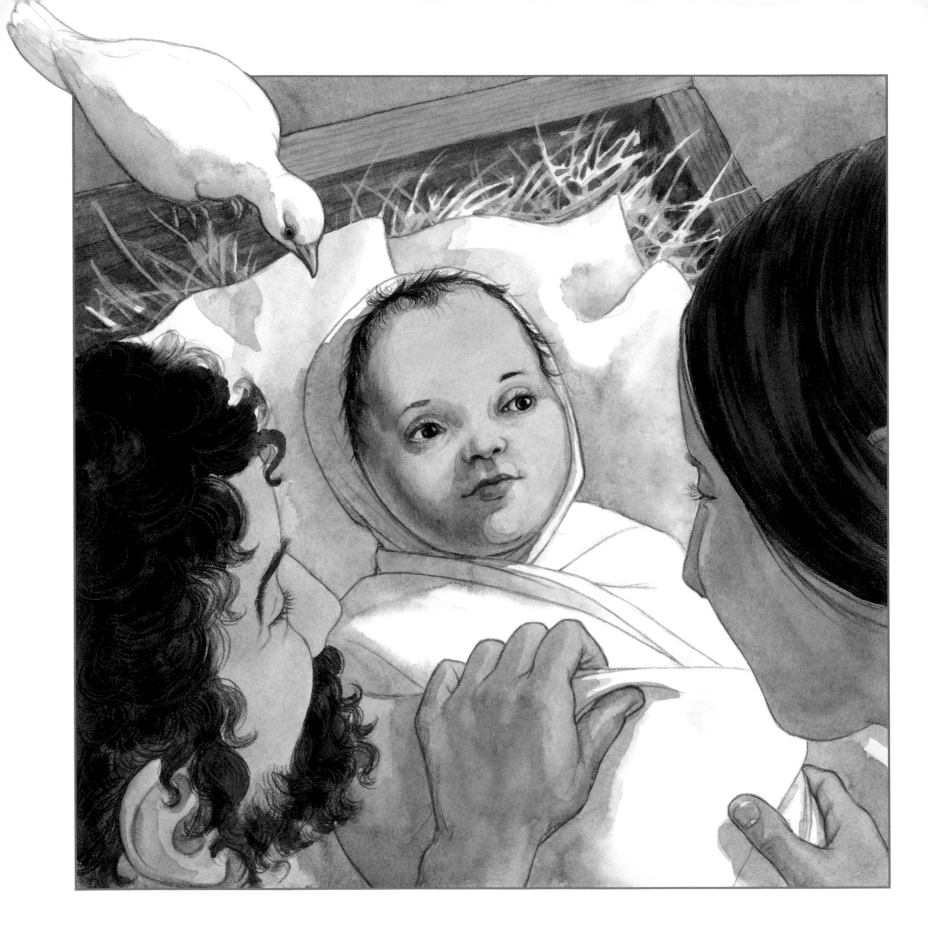

"As for his looks," the dove went on,

"He was a handsome boy.

He had a special warmth to him

That filled the barn with joy.

"Now where was I?" the dove inquired.

"Oh, yes, now I recall.

I told you of this special birth,

But that's not nearly all.

"Soon after Jesus had been born,
Some shepherds came to see.
They called him, 'Savior, Prince of Peace.'
I thought, how can this be?

"How can a baby save the world?
What can a baby do?
And yet I knew, deep in my heart,
The shepherds' words were true.

"An angel had appeared to them
And told them everything.
And then more angels filled the sky
And glorified the King."

"Wow, I wish I'd been there that night!"
The little chicken said.
"I would have praised that baby, too,
And danced around his bed."

"Go on, go on!" the donkey said.
"I want to hear the rest!
My favorite part is coming up,
The part that I like best."

"Which part is that?" asked Mrs. Dove.
"The part about the kings?"
"That's right!" the donkey said and smiled.
"The kings who bring the things."

"That happened later on," said Dove.
"That's what I have been told.
I've heard three kings brought Jesus gifts:
Frankincense, myrrh and gold.

"These men of royalty were wise,"
Explained the aging dove.
"They honored Jesus as God's Son
And gave him gifts of love.

"I love all gifts," the field mouse said,
"Like great, big hunks of cheese.
That's what I would have brought the Lord.
I always aim to please."

"Jesus would not have liked your gift!"
The kid said with a shout.
"I know what I'd have given him.
I've got it figured out."

"Well, what is it?" the field mouse asked.
"What would your gift have been?"
"I'd have given him myself," said Goat,
"To be his bestest friend."

"Me too! Me too!" the colt cried out.
"I would have been his horse.
You think he would have liked that, Dove?"
"Of course," Dove said, "of course."

"But God gave the best gift of all—
He gave his only Son.
And Jesus is for you and me.
He is for everyone."

"Are you quite sure?" the field mouse asked.
"For us?" chimed in the lamb.
"'Cause we're just little animals,
And he's the great 'I Am'."

"That's very true," said Mrs. Dove.

"But God loves you and me.

He'll always love each one of us,

Throughout eternity.

"That's why he sent his Son to earth,"
Explained the wise, old dove.
"That's what Christmas is all about—

"God's never-ending love."